A CHILD'S GARDEN
OF
WEIRDNESS

Illustrations, Verse and Worse

by Dick Gautier

Charles E. Tuttle Company, Inc.
Boston • Rutland, Vermont • Tokyo

A CHILD'S GARDEN
OF
WEIRDNESS

To Pam

Published by the Charles E. Tuttle Company, Inc. of Rutland, Vermont & Tokyo, Japan, with editorial offices at 77 Central Street, Boston, Massachusetts 02109.

Library of Congress Cataloging-in-Publication Data
Gautier, Dick.
    A child's garden of weirdness: illustrations, verse, and worse/by Dick Gautier.
        p.   cm.
        Includes index.
        Summary: Weird poems to amuse and amaze the reader.
        ISBN 0-8048-1825-8
        1. Children's poetry, American. [1. American poetry.] I. Title.
PS3557. A953C48   1993
811'.54—dc20   92-43033
                                                                            CIP
                                                                            AC

Book design by Janis Owens

ISBN 0 8048 1825 8
First printing 1993
PRINTED IN HONG KONG

Magic Carpet

Let's weave a magic carpet with words and thoughts and phrases
Then take the unexplored path that amuses and amazes
Tales and poems that are bizarre, or silly, weird or rare
Leave your normal, formal thoughts behind you if you dare
Hop aboard and we will fly
Out to the brink of where we think
Beyond that furthest patch of sky
Just you and I

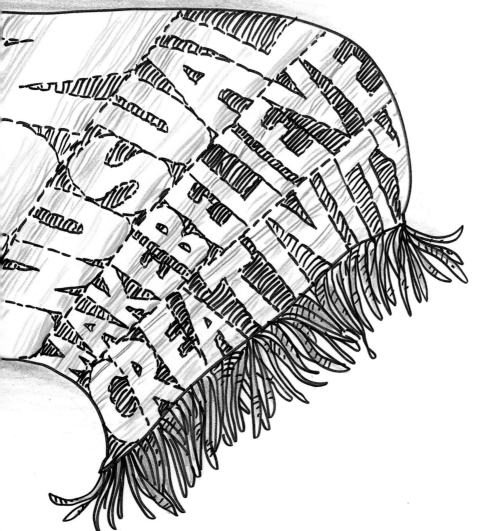

Wake Up Early

Try waking up early in the night
Get up and brush your lips
Iron and dry clean all your hair
Place your feet upon your hips

Stand up straight while bending down
Stoop to touch the ceiling
Or run away while standing still
It's a quite unusual feeling

Stand up then quick! grab your lap
Before it disappears
Then kiss yourself upon the forehead
Or try to join your ears

If you tried to do these silly things
Before you even tested them
Then you are just as weird
As the person who suggested them

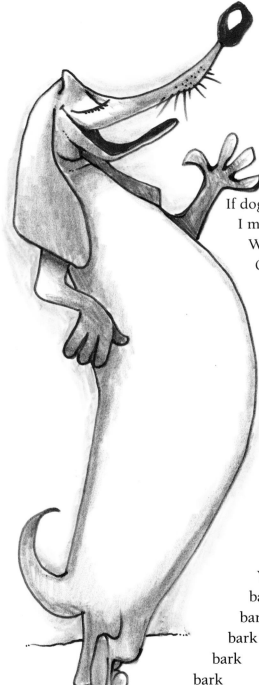

If Dogs Could Talk

If dogs could talk how would that be?
 I mean if they could really converse
  Would it really be better?
   Or worse would it be a curse?

  They could tell you that your mother called
   Or who came by that day
    They could tell you jokes and discuss the news
    And give you comfort but then they . . .

    Might chat about this and that and the cat
    And gab the whole day away
    But I think if dogs could really talk
    This is what they'd say:

    "Pet me, walk me, scratch me, feed me,
    Throw ball, let's go to park"

    You know what? I think I prefer just
     bark
      bark
       bark
      bark
     bark

9

Is Life Boring?

Well, what'll we do today gang? Are we restless, is life boring?
TV is dull, we're tired of games, outside the sky is pouring
Let's change the calendar around, to show you what I mean
Let me see . . . it's April? Great! So we'll celebrate Halloween

Get gauze from the bathroom cabinet, remove it very neatly
Now wrap it all about your head (and I mean completely)
Of course leave room around your nose (it's nice to get some air)
Cover everything except your eyes (yes, even all your hair)
When you're done . . . stand straight and still (this really is a trip)
Do you know what you are? Of course . . . a humongous Q-Tip

Now let's look around some more
What else can we find
That we can use for our masquerade
(But make sure Mom won't mind)
Stick your knees into your shoes,
Then kneel and play the part
Shove your hand inside your coat
And you're Napoleon Bonaparte

Boys, wear a black bathing suit (Girls, a one piece will do)
Then find black gloves, slip on black shoes (Do you even have a clue?)
Stand up straight, stick out your arms and spread your legs apart
Presto! You're the five of spades (now tell me that's not art)

Put glasses on backwards and you're a werewolf with bad eyes
Wear books like shoes and you're 'Frankenstein', a wonderful disguise
Paint numbers all around your face, try not to get too dirty
Hang licorice sticks out of your mouth, you're a clock face at 6:30
Use a danish for a bowtie, a marshmallow for a nose
Put on dad's or mom's things and you're a midget buying clothes
So when you're bored and itchy, just rearrange the year
Do Easter in October, and in June spread Christmas cheer

See? It's easy to leave boredom behind
If you use your mind

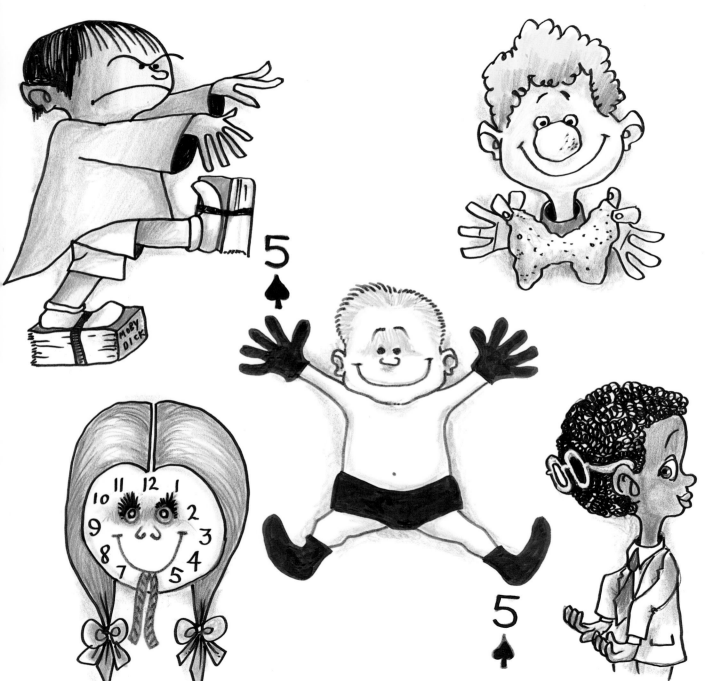

The Shadows

The shadows are dark and ragged
Things swing and catch in my hair
Slowly I make my way forward
A strange odor fills the air

Tangled things tug at my feet
I trip and rip my clothes
I leap over heaps of alien things
There sure are plenty of those

Finally I spot daylight ahead
Behind me lies the gloom
Yes, once again I've done it
I made it through my room

(I'll clean it up someday)

Juggly Bear

A bear that was cuddly
and snuggly
Found some pine cones
and started to juggly
He'd have been okay if
He had noticed the cliff
(I won't tell you the rest, it's
too ugly)

15

English

English is the weirdest language
It sets up rules then breaks them
It gives you all these liberties
Then turns around and takes them

We've spoken it since we were kids
We know its ins and outs
Its twists and turns and maybes
Its dips and dives and doubts

Illogically logical English
With rules that change and shift
If there's boysenberry, why's there no
Girlsenberry? Get my drift?

And here are some more inconsistencies of
Englishese
Listen to these if you please

You can HOP aboard a freighter
But when you JUMP ship you leave
You can laugh until your sides are split
Or laugh right up your sleeve

You clear the road, it's cleared
You fear, yesterday you feared
You hear but then you heard, not heared
English is plenty weird

You may sing, sang and sung
But bring and brought, no brang or brung
We break and so it's broken
With take, we say I took it
And never it was token
If shorts are called shorts, why aren't pants called longs
We can have longer shorts and shorter shorts
There's definitely something wrong

I buy a thing so yesterday I bought
I cry today, past tense should be I crought?
If I cry today then yesterday I cried
If I buy something then yesterday I buyed?

Yes, English is crazy so what's the solution?
Find a different language and avoid the confusion

Lithuanian?
That'd be a painian

Thai?
Don't even try

Norse?
Worse

Let's forget another tongue
And stick with our good old Mother Tongue

Buford

Buford was a wonderful cat
He used the litter box
He was affectionate and playful
And never chewed our socks

He ate his food up promptly
Never howled like some I've heard
He was almost, in fact, the perfect cat
But 'almost' is the operative word

Buford had a little quirk
Not that he wasn't pleasant
The only thing with Buford was
He loved to bring us 'presents'

Things like rotten field mice
Or partially eaten gophers
He'd trot them in and bury them
In the corner of the sofa

We'd find them there after several days
They weren't hard to find
We'd take them out and bury them
But their essence stayed behind

Things'd be fine for a day or two
The odor would start to lift
But then here would come our Buford
With an even more glorious gift

I guess when he saw us bury it
His cat mind seemed to figure
We rejected it because of its size
So he'd go and bring back something bigger

One Easter he dragged in an entire horse
Limp and smelly and dead of course
The authorities came and took it away
But Buford was out the very next day
Looking for another 'gift'
This was causing a rift

Then Buford found the morgue, it wasn't his usual beat
I guess he was just out on the prowl for bigger and better meat
He was trying to find something we wouldn't bury or remove
Wouldn't you know! He brought in a dead guy, Buford had something
to prove

The body had been preserved like morticians always do
No odor thank goodness, however the face was grayish blue
So we had a family huddle and decided there and then
That we'd prop him up, in appropriate clothes, in the corner of our den

So now we're the perfect family
And Buford's the perfect cat
No more scouting around for gifts
He's given up all that

Our new 'uncle' is a treasure
He's so quiet, he takes no food
But the main thing is he shows Buford
Our undying gratitude

The Library

The library's a special place
Where you can find a magic space
And it's so very quiet
That even if you sigh, it
Echoes around the room
Like a breathy sonic boom

I look at all those books on the shelves
And think about all the people themselves
That sat right here and took
Their time reading this very book

And I think of the thousands of people
It took to write them, to bind them
To print them, to find them
To list them, to feed them
To the hungry shelves that need them
Just so I can sit here
And read them
With the silence all around me
In the library

Tacos

Tacos are the perfect food
They contain four basic food groups
Meat, dairy, vegetable, grain
And they're tastier than Froot Loops

The only thing about tacos is
You can't eat them while erect
You have to twist your body around
And dislocate your neck

Except for that one little kink
I think
Tacos are the perfect food

23

Coin a Word

Have you ever burped and sneezed at once?
No? Well, it happens anyhow
There's no actual word for this
So let's coin one here and now

In the future if you sneeze and burp
Smile sweetly and say "Please,
Excuse me, I didn't mean to 'snurp'
Or perhaps I should say 'beeze'"

Coining words is lots of fun
Let's think of more to do
Like . . . I don't think there is a word
For wriggling into your shoe

How about 'squipping'? What do you think?
Is that something you'd do with shoes?
Or "I 'fraished' into my sneakers"
There's a good one we could use

And you know that sound your stomach makes
When you're hungry for some food?
It's like a distant liquid growl
It's not exactly rude

A muffled gurgle like deep inside
You uncorked a drain
What do you think of 'gruzzling'
Or think of a better name

Try 'bloobering' or 'swerbling'
Or you know what's really best?
Forget mine, coin your own word
And put it to the test

Use the word with all your friends
And who knows, its use could grow
Till one day it could be as well known
As stomach or hello

And maybe, many years from now
When you're turning gray
Someone will remind you
Of that very special day

When you created your own word
That now everybody knows
Yes, you've added to our language
A nice feeling, I suppose

The Human Body

The human body is a wonderful machine
It can fuel up and dispose of waste
You know what I mean

But if I had the power to change
To rearrange our features
I'd place our mouths atop our heads
It would make us superior creatures

Before you write me off as bats
Just think for a minute, how neat
It would be to stick food in our hats
And eat going down the street

We could sing as loud as we wanted
And never be heard out there
Or talk to ourselves the whole day long
And no one'd point or stare

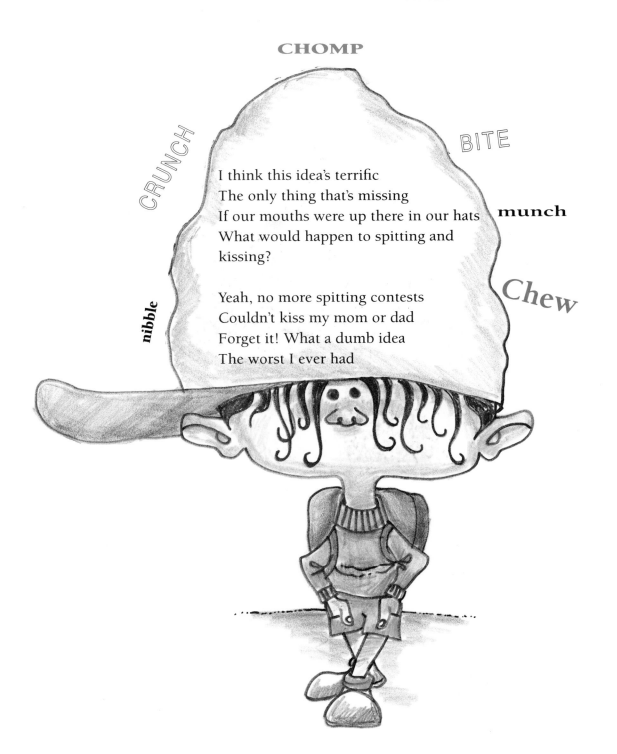

CHOMP

CRUNCH

BITE

munch

Chew

nibble

I think this idea's terrific
The only thing that's missing
If our mouths were up there in our hats
What would happen to spitting and
kissing?

Yeah, no more spitting contests
Couldn't kiss my mom or dad
Forget it! What a dumb idea
The worst I ever had

Talking Backwards

Talking backwards is really fun, I wish we'd do more of it
If we said DOOF instead of FOOD, I think everyone would love it
KNITS would come out sounding STINK and MARK would come out
KRAM
APRIL would be LIRPA and MAY . . . what else but YAM

Politicians should do it, just a few words every day
It'd probably make as much sense as what they usually say
CALIFORNIA'd be AINROFILAC, and NEW YORK'd be KROY WEN
And who knows if we all laughed together, we might see daylight again

Maybe we'd get along better, if talking backwards was the rule
And we all could live in CEEP again; let's try it, what can we ZOOL?

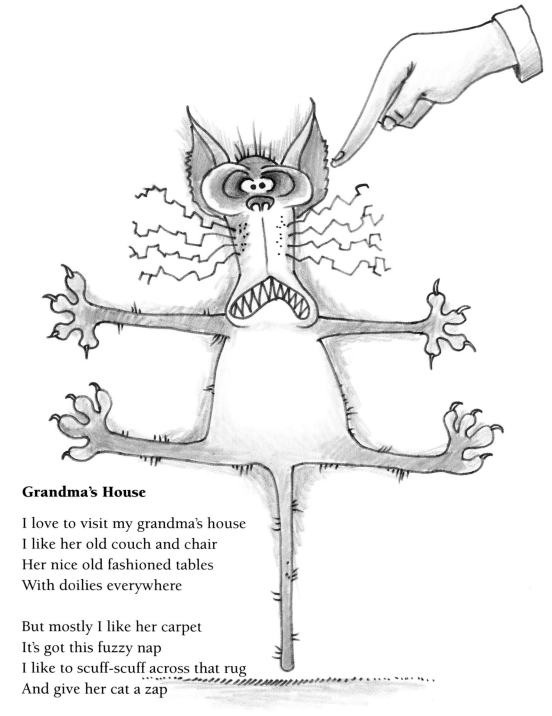

Grandma's House

I love to visit my grandma's house
I like her old couch and chair
Her nice old fashioned tables
With doilies everywhere

But mostly I like her carpet
It's got this fuzzy nap
I like to scuff-scuff across that rug
And give her cat a zap

Carlin P. Trump

Carlin P. Trump was a boy but a grump
Who would snarl at his friends and his folks
He'd complain all the while and never a smile
And he never would laugh at your jokes

Carlin P. had no pal, no buddy, no gal
His parents were hard pressed to love him
He was so darned unpleasant that anyone present
Wanted to punch him or shove him

He didn't seem to mind, he was cross and unkind
Then one night when he was showering
He had just rinsed his hair when he stopped and he stared
And for a second he almost stopped glowering

A small patch of hair was suddenly there
It kind of . . . just sort of . . . appeared
Where before there was, not one bit of fuzz
Something was growing . . . and weird

He shrugged and thought "Well . . . you never can tell
It'll probably be gone by the morning"
He couldn't have known, that that tuft that had grown
Was, in fact, a sinister warning

Trump went on with his life, causing gloom, causing strife
He always made his parents worry
Then one day in the gym, Carlin got grim
Cause the boys laughed at his back turning furry

It grew even worse, this strange hairy curse
His nose turned much darker, and shiny
His hands even changed, his ears rearranged
And now his hair was thicker and spiny

Carlin became aware, he was turning into a **b e a r**
A small but dark brown, furry, teddy
He thought "Can this be? What's happening to me?
I don't want to be a bear, I'm not ready"

He tried acting nice, he smiled (even twice)
He greeted folks to their surprise
But it was too late, this was Carlin's fate
Now Carlin had small bearish eyes

Well the change was complete, he had paws, furry feet
You almost couldn't tell him from Smoky
He had a black shiny nose, could barely wear his clothes
He looked like a real bear . . . only hokey

He decided what to do, he'd have to join the zoo
He lumbered through the night and found their cage
But every single bear chased him out of there
"Now where to turn?" he cried out with rage

"I know", he thought, "of course, I'll go live in the forest
Why it's the perfect place for any bear"
So he wandered through the glade, thinking "Hey, I've got it made"
He'd forgot about the others living there

A group of real bears stood and checked him out but good
"I'd like to join you", he said with a sniff
They huddled for a sec, then grabbed him by the neck
And said "Okay but there's one great big IF

"Bears have this crummy name, for being cross. We're not to blame
You can stay but remember you're on trial"
If he proved himself he would be allowed to stay for good
The catch was that he ALWAYS had to smile

Now it's hard for bears to grin, they're not exactly thin
Those fat cheeks make it difficult at best
But smile Carlin does, through his brownish bearish fuzz
His jaws ache but he's got to pass this test

He smiles and he smiles, his teeth they gleam for miles
This constant toothy grin does he project
All the while the bears are snarlin' at super smiling Carlin
The shoe's on the other foot now I suspect

So if you're camping out some spring, don't think you're seeing things
If a bear comes by flashing a phony smile
It's only you-know-who still paying up his dues
And he'll be doing it for quite a little while

I guess I should mention, no one back home paid much attention
The school didn't call, life went marching on
A month later his Mom said "S'pose Carlin's in his bed?"
It's pretty bad when no one cares you're gone

Yes, Carlin P. Trump was a definite grump
Now he must be pleasant and serve
He's paying the piper, with that smile (looking hyper)
I guess he got what he deserved

Dangerous Journey

We had to put on these special boots
And get all set for climbing
It's a rough and dangerous job up there
It requires perfect timing

We started out bright and early
When the world was half awake
We arrived at the foot pretty tired
So we took a doughnut break

That spooky rumbling that we heard
Was not some distant thunder
It came from the giant mountain
From somewhere way deep under

Carefully we made our way
One step then another
I looked over and there was sweat
On the face of my little brother

We pushed ahead, we had to
It took all the guts we had
But that is what you have to do

If
you
want
to
climb
Mt. Dad

Coloring

Here's one of the things I like to do
When things just couldn't be duller
I dig out my good old coloring book
And crayons with which to color

I use purple for the faces
And yellow for the eyes
I make the flowers black and grey
And pink and red for the skies

When I'm all done I sign it
The 'Ts' I cross, the 'Is' I dot 'em
And then I sign my sister's name
Right at the very bottom

Afraid of the Dark

Some kids are afraid of the dark
But I think the dark is a friend
Who comes around to tell us that day's about to end

It paints a purple background so we can see the stars
And the glowing moonlight shadows that frolic in our yards

When morning comes, it packs its purple cloak and then
Greets the sun, steps aside and tiptoes out again
I think the dark is a friend

Barber Jim

Jim is a great barber and a good guy
I sit in his chair and I never ever cry
Like some of the other kids
I don't think I ever did

He never stuck me accidentally with his sharp scissors
But his floor looks like there was a hair blizzard
Jim asks me how I like school and I say "Fine"
He asks me that every single time

Jim looks at my mom and smiles and winks
And no one ever sees him flirt . . . he thinks
When I'm done Jim lifts me out of the chair
And gives me a big red sucker all covered with hair

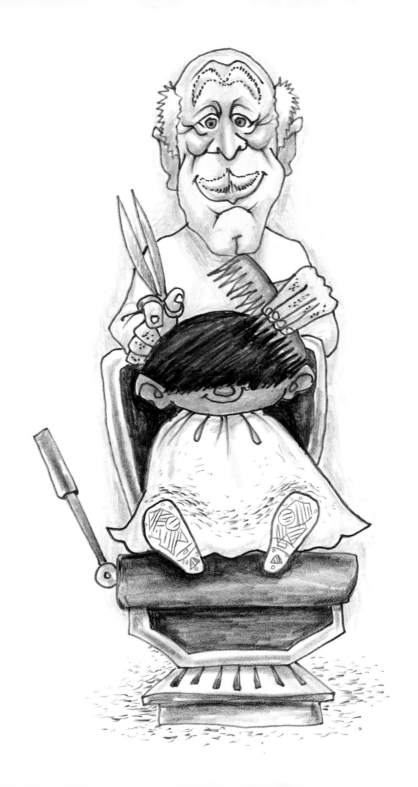

Secret Place

I know a very secret place
Where no one ever goes
Where I can hide without a trace
In this place that no one knows

You'll never find it, I'm not kiddin'
Even if you are a whiz
But this place is so well hidden
Even I don't know where it is

The Playground

The playground is a lovely place
Where I can run and race and chase
But then I fell and bent my face
The playground is an ugly place

41

Halloween

Of all the holidays my favorite's Halloween
I can dress up like big brother
Act like him and be mean

I make fun of him and he can't slug me
Or do anything else to bug me

I wear my sneakers untied and sloppy
And a beat up baseball cap
And I walk real low and cool, you know
I chew gum and make it snap
And my pants are way down below my waist
He has no taste

Oh here comes my brother now . . . but wait
He can't, he's wearing my clothes
Short pants, a T-shirt and look at that
He's drawn freckles on his nose
This isn't how it's supposed to be
He's wearing glasses and he looks like me

Remember when I said Halloween was the best
holiday?
No way

The Movies

Isn't going to the movies great?
Get tickets, stand in line and wait
And talk to friends and laugh
and then
The line begins to move again

You get inside of course to find
Another long and winding line
For popcorn, candy, and drinks so you
Get one of each . . . and a hot dog, too

Now look around and find your seats
And you settle down and drink and eat
And chat until the lights grow dark
And the movie's about to start

But we've eaten and drunk, we've had our fun
Aw . . . let's go home, I saw this one

Designer Kids

Some kids that I call unstable
Think they're hot (this is not just a fable)
They look down their noses
Wear designer clotheses
Heck, why don't they wear just the label?

Dinosaurs

All the dinosaurs upped and disappeared
Without a word, isn't that kind of weird?
To this very day no one knows why
And lots of famous scientists gave it a try

No one has an answer, not even a guess
Of course dinosaurs leave no forwarding address

But they didn't have sports or cable shows
Or fast food places or Nintendos
Or movies or parks or barbeques
They all wandered around in the primordial ooze

I don't know if anyone's thought of it
You think maybe they just got bored and split?

47

Frederic

In the icy depths of the Northern sea
Where the water's cold and clear
Lived a creature name of Frederic
Who filled no one with fear

Frederic was a friendly soul
Sweet and nice and affable
He liked to laugh and tell old jokes
He was so mild it was laughable

But the other creatures from the dark
Didn't like . . . Frederic the Friendly Funny Shark

He was just too soft and sensitive
He couldn't get in the swim
Of acting like a savage beast
It simply wasn't him

He never ate a bite of seafood
He considered that too vicious
Fred was a vegetarian
And found seaweed delicious

He was snubbed by the other sharks
Who warned "Shape up or split"
So Freddy roamed the Seven Seas
Looking for a place he'd fit

Frederic the Friendly Funny Shark
Who liked to kid and joke
Who liked to romp and have a lark
Who warmed to human folk

Our Fred was much too trusting
As he swam towards a boat
A harpoon flew and caught him
Right there in the throat

He thrashed around but that harpoon
Cut off his dorsal fin
His teeth got smashed and to boot
His nose got beaten in

But he escaped and nursed his wounds
Beneath a cloudless sky
When he saw his reflection
He said "Who is that guy?"

His nose was no longer like a shark's
Nor his teeth, nor his fin, nor his mouth
Then our Frederic got a brainstorm
And started swimming south

Fred works at Sea World to this day
As a technical advisor
With his new nose and teeth no more fin
No one is the wiser

Which goes to show you things are not
Always what they seem to be
It's hard to face
But it's a good case
For cosmetic surgery

Dog House

I built a house for our dog Joe
And I didn't even need my dad
I found a bunch of old used boards
I used all the nails we had

I showed it to Joe but he wouldn't go in
Well it was a little rickety
He flattened his ears down on his head
And acted so persnickety

I shoved him in but he looked real sad
And then made his getaway
He hid under the porch all that night
And part of the following day

After all my work. How do you like that?
You think maybe I could rent it to the cat?

Cuss Words

Don't use the same old cuss words that everybody uses
Come up with new and different ones, and some that might amuse us
If you happen to step on a tack shout out 'Birgaloo'
If you stub your toes say 'Mankalay' or 'Jellicameroo'
When you get mad say 'Cratzna prodo', 'Holy Bellaschmare'
Or scream 'Arechs' or maybe 'Nindunne', or even 'Splessonair'

'Dardlefain' or 'Penderfink'
'Jenor', 'Maltications'
They're not just fun to say but think . . .
they're
your
very
own
creations

PLETZ

MARKEN

SNARF

PEELOT

Gerald

Gerald's hobby (if you can call it that) was to gross out other kids
He loved acting disgusting, it's about all he ever did
His nose was a favorite source from which to have some fun
He'd flick the contents on the wall and then when he was done
He'd spit, how Gerald loved to spit
Wherever and whenever he could
Up in the air, on the ground, in trees, on dirt, on wood

At dinner, he'd chew up all his food
Then open his mouth real wide
Gerald was what you call super-crude
That cannot be denied

He used most of his bodily fluids
To do things I cannot mention
Well he didn't feel smart or funny
How else could he get attention?

He got punished but five minutes later
He was up to his old tricks
His parents finally gave up hope
His friends they just got sick

Then one day a new kid came to school
The kids dubbed him Jabba the Hut
He was eight years old but a number one slob
And he had a big fat sloppy gut

For lunch he had three chickens and inhaled them in a sec
And it looked like he had something blackish brown growing on his
neck
When he ate, food dripped from his lips and landed on his clothes
During which he never stopped digging around in his nose

That's the best thing that happened to Gerald
A stroke of incredible luck
When Gerald saw him up close, disgusting and gross
A new word sprang from his lips

He

said

"Yuck"

Seen and Not Heard

"Children should be seen and not heard"
I hear grownups say that often
But think about it, not a word?
We'd be quieter than a coffin

Playgrounds would be just like tombs
No cheering during sports
And how about our classrooms
You mean no more oral reports?

And when we fell and scraped our knees
From wrestling on the couch
No one'd know we were hurt, you see
Because we couldn't yell "Ouch"

It's silly not to say a word
There's a very good way to show 'em
If children were seen and not heard
Who would be reading this poem?

Marguerite

Marguerite was petite and quite sweet
But boy did she have big feet
It seemed that everyone she met,
wouldn't let her forget
The enormity of her deformity

She tried dance class once but
she had to quit
She split
all of her shoes
Marguerite felt doomed to constant ridicule
By her friends, her family, everyone at school
Marguerite had the big foot blues

It was hard for her parents, too
There were certain things they had to do
Like it took an entire crew
To make one single Marguerite shoe

Marguerite and her family lived out on the prairie
Where the winds blew hard and sometimes it was scary
But little did she know that one giant blow
Was coming to make her life different (and very)

A tornado appeared right out of the blue
Like the one in the Wizard of Oz
And it blew and it blew at the houses which flew
Around wildly like small bits of gauze

It swept down and picked up Marguerite's farm
And the cows and the sheep who were sleeping
When her family appeared, the wind (as she feared)
Grabbed them too and continued its sweeping

But Marguerite she didn't budge, she simply stood firm on the farm
Yes, her huge feet held her there and kept her from harm
She acted quite heroically, she fought the storm off stoically
And she held the others in her family fast
Until the storm had passed
And there was quiet again at last

Marguerite was an instant celebrity
(Which she secretly wished to be)
CBS, ABC, NBC, CNN
Came to interview her, she was famous but then
So was Rudolph and others of stories of old
Who took their drawbacks and turned them to gold

But this isn't the end of Marguerite's tale, no not
By a longshot

It was fine for awhile, she was greeted with smiles
But soon her brave feat was forgotten
And it wasn't soon after, her feet caused more laughter
Marguerite thought "This is rotten"

So she had a real temper tantrum
She stomped about, she was infuriated
The Richterscales thumped, seismologists jumped
The poor town was nearly annihilated

Yes, that was about it
For the town and all because
Their Marguerite was
Having a snit

They almost paid the price but it turned the townsfolk nice
From that day every soul was so polite
They'd greet Marguerite with "Hi there" and "Sweet"
And generally treated her right

The town knew if they made her feel bad some way
Those lethal legs she'd unleash
And before you could say "Have a nice day"
The town would be history . . . Capish?

So things have calmed down in Margueritown
(They renamed it to curry her favor)
Even ice cream shops renamed all their stock
They're now all 31 'Marguerite' flavor

Finally Marguerite feels complete
Isn't that neat?

Tie Your Shoes

Sammy hated to tie his shoelaces
So he'd trip in the stupidest places
When he fell in the mall
His nose broke his fall
This'll give you a hint how his face is. . .

Index by Title